Starry Forest Books, Inc. • P.O. Box 1797, 217 East 70th Street, New York, NY 10021 • Starry Forest is a trademark of Starry Forest Books, Inc. • Text and Illustrations © 2017 by Starry Forest Books, Inc. • This 2017 edition published by Starry Forest Books, Inc. • All rights reserved. No part of this publication may be reproduced, stored in a retrieval system, or transmitted in any form or by any means (including electronic, mechanical, photocopying, recording, or otherwise) without prior written permission from the publisher. • ISBN 978-1-946260-03-1 • Manufactured in Huizhou City, Guangdong Province, China • Lot #: 2 4 6 8 10 9 7 5 3 1 • 07/17

CLASSIC STORIES

Robin Hood

retold by
Peter Clover

illustrated by
Marcin Piwowarski

Long ago in the heart of England, a young man named Robin Hood was walking through Sherwood Forest. Robin was a great archer. No one in the land could compete with his perfect aim.

Richard I, King of England, owned Sherwood Forest. But King Richard was away fighting in the Crusades. His nasty brother, Prince John, was ruling in his place. Prince John hired foresters to catch poachers like Robin Hood, who hunted in Sherwood Forest.

Suddenly, Robin came across a party of Prince John's foresters.
One of the men was jealous of Robin Hood's growing fame,
and decided to trick him.

He pointed to a deer in the distance and taunted Robin, "No one can strike a target that far away. Especially not a young man like you!"

This made Robin very angry. Without thinking, he drew his bow and fired an arrow that struck the deer in the blink of an eye.

The forester smiled. "Now you will hang, for killing one of the king's deer."
Robin fled, but the forester chased him deep into the forest, firing arrows as he
ran. Robin Hood had no choice but to fight back. He sent an arrow flying into
the forester's heart. Robin escaped, but Prince John put a price on his head.
Robin Hood was now an outlaw.

Other men began living in Sherwood Forest. Prince John's unfair laws and taxes had forced these men to leave their homes. Just like Robin Hood, these outlaws were loyal to King Richard. They wore Lincoln green and formed a merry band with Robin as their leader. Together, they robbed from the rich and gave to the poor.

One day, as Robin was about to cross a stream, a giant man stepped onto the other end of the fallen log.

"Go back and let me pass," said the stranger.

Robin placed an arrow in his bow and smiled. "It is you, my friend, that will go back and let me pass!"

"Only a coward would shoot a man armed with only a wooden staff!" said the stranger.

Robin was anything but a coward. And he loved a challenge, so he cut himself a staff of oak, and stepped back onto the bridge.

"Now we are equal," he said. "Let's see who falls first."

Robin Hood was an expert with the staff, but so was the stranger.
And he was much bigger than Robin, with the strength of a bull.
He knocked Robin off the log with a terrific blow, and stood there
laughing as Robin sat in the bubbling stream.

Robin blew his hunting horn, and was immediately surrounded by his
Merry Men. The stranger was shocked when he realized who Robin was.

But Robin admired the skill of this giant man. "What is your name?" he asked.

"John Little," came the reply. The Merry Men roared with laughter.

"Such a funny name for such a big man," said Robin. "Come join our merry band, Little John. And let us call you a friend."

Determined to catch Robin Hood, the Sheriff of Nottingham decided to organize an archery tournament. He hoped the prize of a golden arrow would lure Robin out of hiding.

Robin, not knowing about the trick, entered the sheriff's competition.
He traveled with his three best men—Will Scarlet, Alan a Dale, and Little
John. Disguised as peasants, they would enter Nottingham unrecognized.

First, they needed to cross the River Maun. A friar named Tuck was standing
at the shore. Robin offered Friar Tuck a gold coin to carry him across the river.
He made the friar carry him not once, not twice, but three times back and forth.
Finally, Friar Tuck grew impatient and dropped Robin into the river.

Robin was furious. He chased Friar Tuck all the way to the friary,
where the two men grappled. Robin admired the friar's free spirit, so he
asked him to join their merry band and help the poor. Friar Tuck,
who hated Prince John's high taxes, agreed.

The Sheriff of Nottingham was sure Robin Hood would appear
at the archery tournament. But since Robin and his men were disguised,
the sheriff did not know that Robin was there.

One of the sheriff's men was favored to win the golden arrow. He shot
an arrow that struck the center of the target.

It seemed impossible for anyone to beat the shot. Out of the crowd, came Robin Hood. He was stooped over like an old man, with his head covered by a hood. The sheriff laughed. Surely this old man was joking.

Robin Hood lifted his bow and placed his arrow. The arrow from the sheriff's archer was still in the center of the target. Friar Tuck hushed the crowd as Robin took aim. Robin let his arrow fly and it raced to the target, splitting the other arrow's shaft from feather to head.

The crowd held its breath in wonder. Then the sheriff cried, "That's Robin Hood!" He jumped up from his seat, pointing to where the mysterious archer had been standing. But Robin and his men had vanished, along with their prize, the golden arrow. Friar Tuck had slipped it up his baggy sleeve.

When Maid Marian saw Robin shoot his arrow, she fell in love with the outlaw and his adventurous life. Marian secretly stole away into Sherwood Forest, dressed in the clothes of a young boy. It didn't take her long to find Robin Hood.

Without speaking, Maid Marian drew a sword and challenged Robin to fight. Robin quickly overpowered her. When he pulled off her hood and saw that she was a beautiful girl, he immediately fell in love.

Robin and his merry band continued helping the poor, including a knight named Sir Richard of Lea. Sir Richard was deeply in debt to the Abbot of St. Mary's at York. If he did not pay the debt within the week, the abbot would seize all his land.

Robin was deeply moved by Sir Richard's plight, so he gave the knight the money he needed. News of Robin's kindness spread to distant lands.

At last, King Richard returned from the Crusades. The entire kingdom rejoiced. When the king heard of Robin Hood's great deeds he decided to meet Robin for himself, to test his valor and honor.

Disguised as a friar, King Richard found Robin Hood in the forest. Robin, fooled by the disguise, invited the friar to dine with him. They talked about many things, and Robin spoke of his loyalty to King Richard and to England.

King Richard was curious if Robin Hood was as good with a bow
and arrow as the stories told. Robin was happy to show off his skill,
so he picked a tree as his target and let an arrow fly.

The arrow missed.

Robin was embarrassed and furious. He asked the friar to punish him
for the terrible shot. The friar knocked him on the head with his fist.
Robin's Merry Men roared with laughter.

"How would you feel," King Richard asked Robin, "if the king granted you a royal pardon, and invited you to join the king's men?"

"That is something I wish more than anything in the world," answered Robin.

The friar stood up with a majestic air. "I am King Richard of England. And I hereby grant you and your men a royal pardon."

At the sight of their king, Robin and his men knelt before him.

"Arise," said the king. "No longer outlaws, you are free to leave the forest and serve your king and country."

Robin Hood and his merry men served the king faithfully, and Robin became chief of the king's soldiers. He never missed another shot.

One beautiful day in May, Robin married his sweetheart, Maid Marian.
And together, they had many adventures.